GIRLS WHO BELONG TO OTHER MEN
BOOK 1
PETE ANDREWS

This is a work of fiction. ***All characters are of legal age and are 18 years old or older.***

First Edition. October 2023.

ABOUT THE AUTHOR

I used to publish under *xleglover* and *Flash of Stocking* on various sites.

My stories are romances, so they explore the feelings, emotions, and relationships of the characters. My stories have an emotional edge to them. The characters have thrilling adventures, but there's pain there too, at least for some of them.

I try to write stories that seem like real life. Yes, the situations are extreme, but I hope you come away thinking, *"Yes, I can see how that might happened."*

You can find my books at **Amazon Kindle** and **Smashwords**. Also, **Barnes & Noble, Apple Books,** and **Rakuten kobo**. If you'd like to join my mailing list or would like to send me a question or feedback, please email me at *peteandrews1701@gmail.com.*

BOOKS BY PETE ANDREWS

Faithful Wife's Fall From Grace (on-going series)

Book 1
Book 2
Book 3
Book 4

Girls Who Belong To Other Men (2 book series)

Book 1
Book 2

Opening Pandora's Box (5 book series)

Book 1: Jessie Plays For Her Husband
Book 2: Ollie Watches His Wife With Another Man
Book 3: Jessie Grows Closer To Roman
Book 4: Jessie Loses Herself In Roman
Book 5: How Can You Do This To Me?

Available at Amazon Kindle and Smashwords.

CHAPTER 1

It started my first semester in college. I ran into Suzanne, a girl I knew from home. We ran in the same social circles in high school, but never interacted that much. She was always with Fred, her long-term boyfriend. But it was nice seeing a friendly face, so we went out for a beer.

One beer led to another, and pretty soon we were both feeling no pain. I walked her home. It started pouring as we reached her dorm, so she invited me in. Her roommate was away for the weekend visiting her boyfriend. We laughed drinking beer in her dorm room as the rain turned into a thunderstorm.

I'd never been interested in Suzanne. Not that she was a dog or anything. In fact she was pretty, with brown hair and a very cute, sweet face. She had big tits. Fred always raved about them whenever the guys got together. She was a little chubby though (I guess she'd be called pleasantly plump). Her legs were decent but not great.

I've always been more into skinny girls with long hair and great legs. So I never really thought much about her in high school.

And to be fair, she never gave me the time of day either. Like I said, she was committed to Fred. All through high school, they talked about getting married after college, and I figured that was still their plan.

But here we were together with it pouring outside. With my brain fogged by beer, Suzanne started to look good. On top of that, I think we were both homesick and lonely. So around midnight, with the rain still pounding against the window, I leaned over and kissed her.

She resisted at first, but I persisted, having gone an entire week without pussy. I thrust my tongue into her mouth, and eventually she began returning my kisses. I brought my hand between us and felt her tits. Shit they were big. I massaged her breast meat and rubbed her nipples. When she started moaning, I knew she wouldn't stop me unbuttoning her blouse.

She wore a plain tan bra with a front clasp. I opened it and gazed at her bare breasts. I'm not a tit man, but hers looked pretty good, shapely with just a little sag, and capped with enormous erect nipples. For a moment I envied Fred. Having these to play with all the time? Not the worst thing in the world.

I caressed Suzanne's soft flesh of her left breast, and leaned down and sucked her right nipple. She responded, moaning and arching her back. Pretty soon I had her writhing under me.

I moved my hands down to her jeans. As I began tugging them off, Suzanne put her hands on mine, stopping me. "I can't," she said between gasps. "I love Fred."

I knew it was a dick move. Suzanne was Fred's girl, and Fred was my buddy. But at that point, I was too horny to stop.

I kissed Suzanne and fondled her tits. I kissed her neck, caressed her breasts, thumbed her nipples, ran my hands down her back. I used all the tricks in my bag to get her super-hot so she would forget about Fred, at least until I got my dick inside her.

With one of her nipples in my mouth – her nipples were super sensitive, I could tell—I pulled down her jeans. This time she didn't stop me.

There was a wet spot in her panties. I fingered her and she groaned.

I curled my fingers into her panties and began pulling them down her fleshy thighs.

"Please don't," Suzanne pleaded.

"Fred never needs to know," I promised, kissing her again.

Suzanne kissed me back, and she even raised her ass when I began pulling down her panties again. I figured she was horny for cock. For years she'd probably been getting it regularly from Fred, but that had stopped when college started a few months ago. No sex for 3 months? I can barely last a week. No wonder she was horny.

When I pulled her panties off her feet – and I had to admit, while her legs were on the thick side, she had pretty feet – I took a moment to look at her pussy.

I was surprised to see her completely shaved. Like, full Brazilian. I had always thought of Suzanne as the bohemian-type, an oaks and granola kind of girl. So I expected a full bush. Seeing her bare like that made me realize how much effort she took to keep herself looking nice for Fred. As I looked at her shaved pussy, I thought to myself, "Fred buddy, lucky you, I think you found a winner with Suzanne."

Thinking about Fred didn't mean I wasn't going to fuck his girlfriend. Call me a dick, but the longer this night went along, the more I wanted to sink my man-meat into this chick.

I quickly pulled off my shirt and then tugged down my jeans and shorts. Suzanne's eyes were locked on my cock. I'd seen Fred naked in the gym shower after PE, and I knew I was bigger than him.

I reached into my wallet and pulled out the condom I always kept there. Suzanne watched as I ripped open the package and rolled the latex down my shaft. Her cheeks were flushed, and her eyes were heavy lidded. I could tell this girl was dying to be fucked.

I rubbed my cockhead up and down her slit. Her pussy lips glistened with moisture. As I began pressing into her, she put a palm on my chest to stop me.

"Go slow," Suzanne said.

"I will," I promised. As I got ready to thrust into her, she pushed against me with her palm again.

"You swear you'll never tell Fred?" she asked.

"I swear," I said, leaning down and kissing her. We kissed for a few moments, trading spit as our tongues danced together. Then, with her arms around my neck as we kissed, I pushed my cock into her.

Suzanne gasped as my cock penetrated her. "God ...," she groaned as I pushed deeper into her.

I went slow, taking my time, letting her get used to my length and girth. Finally when I was balls deep, we took a moment. We were looking at each other, panting into each other's face.

"Are you okay?" I asked her.

"Yeah, it's just …," she said, panting. "You're really big."

"I'll be gentle," I said as I began moving in and out. As I began fucking Fred's girlfriend.

As Suzanne got used to my size, she began rocking back and forth with me, getting in sync with my thrusts. I squeezed her big tits and pinched her nipples as I fucked her, making her moan and roll her head back.

We were both getting close to the promised land when Suzanne's phone began ringing. "Oh god no!" she cried seeing the caller ID. "It's Fred!"

"Don't answer," I told her.

"I can't," Suzanne said looking panicked. "We always talk before going to sleep. If I don't answer he'll think something's wrong."

"Pull out," she said, pushing against my chest.

"I'm not pulling out," I told her. I was *not* going to end this night with blue balls.

Suzanne stared at me for long moments. Realizing I was serious, she urgently pleaded "Don't say anything, okay? And stop moving."

When I nodded, Suzanne put the phone to her ear. "Hi baby, um, I miss you so much, what'd you do today?"

I listened as they spoke, supporting myself on my arms. I thought I might grow soft as they spoke, but the wickedness of my cock buried deep inside Suzanne as she talked to Fred was keeping me hard.

I leaned down and nibbled on her neck. She pushed me away and glared at me. I leaned down again and kissed her lips even as she spoke to Fred. As I did, I heard Fred telling her about binging *The Last of Us*.

Suzanne pushed me away again. I reached down and squeezed her big tits. When I rubbed the flats of my thumbs over her nipples, she clenched her teeth to prevent herself from moaning.

"You should watch it," I heard Fred say. "It's as good as *The Walking Dead*."

"I will," Suzanne said with a strained voice. She was frantically shaking her head, trying to get me to stop. I ignored her and continued fondling her breasts. She squeezed her eyes shut, doing all she could to keep from moaning.

It excited me to hear Suzanne trying to carry on a normal conversation with her boyfriend with my cock buried deep inside her. I couldn't resist rocking back and forth. Suzanne's eyes went wide and again she frantically shook her head no.

Again, I ignore her. I slowly thrusted in and out. I was gentle, not pushing deep or hard. And I was quiet. Fred couldn't hear a thing (except maybe Suzanne's heavy breathing). But I was fucking her. While she was on the phone with her boyfriend.

Suzanne tried to talk normally to Fred, but I could tell the fucking was getting to her. I started taking slightly faster, slightly longer strokes, making her face flush with pleasure. Then I reached down and flicked my finger over her clit. This time she couldn't help moaning. Fred heard it.

"What was that, are you okay?" I heard Fred ask.

"Yeah, yeah, I'm okay, I'm just, ah, I'm just a little tired," Suzanne answered. She was panting.

"I really miss you Suzy," Fred said. "This long distance romance thing sucks."

"Yeah," Suzanne said. She was looking in my eyes as I continued to fuck her. She had a desperate, frantic look on her cute chubby face.

"I can't wait until Christmas break," Fred said. "I can't wait to see you."

Suzanne pressed both her hands on my chest. Her eyes begged me to stop.

I decided to be nice. I stopped fucking her, but I didn't pull out.

"I can't wait to see you too," Suzanne said to Fred. She was still breathing hard, but at least now she wasn't getting fucked as she said lovey things to her boyfriend.

"I love you Suzy," Fred said. There was so much emotion in his voice. I heard it, and so did Suzanne. It got me hot that he was professing his love for his girlfriend while she was impaled on my hard cock.

Suzanne's eyes teared up. She was thinking the same thing as me. But while it got me hot, she felt sad and regretful since she was betraying the man she loved.

"I love you too Freddie," Suzanne said. "I guess I better get going. I have an early class tomorrow."

"Okay. Bye. I love you," Fred said.

"I love you too," Suzanne said. Then she pushed the button to end the call.

Suzanne looked into my face. Tears ran down her cheeks. But she didn't tell me to pull out, or try to push me away.

I leaned down and kissed her. She kissed me back, wrapping her arms around my neck.

I began moving in and out again. She gripped my arms as I began fucking her faster and harder.

I put Suzanne's legs on my shoulders, and began to really fuck her. I rammed her pussy hard and fast.

"Oh god, oh god, oh god, oh god ...," she moaned. Her moans were continuous now. I was pretty sure Freddie had never fucked her so hard. Or so good.

I felt Suzanne's pussy squeeze around my cock, and then she was thrashing about as she came. She clamped her hands over her mouth to muffle her screams so her dormmates wouldn't hear her cum.

I wanted to orgasm in Suzanne's pussy. But something came over me. For years in high school, I'd seen them kiss. Suzanne kissing Fred.

I wanted to cum in her mouth. I wanted her lips that kissed Fred all those years wet with my jizz.

So just as I was about to cum, I pulled out. I quickly pulled off the condom and then I moved up to her face. I pushed my cock into her mouth.

I didn't push in too far. I didn't want her to gag. But I held her head tight so she had no choice but to swallow by sperm.

Afterwards I collapsed onto the bed beside her. We both were panting. Our bodies were covered in sweat.

"Please leave," Suzanne said in a quiet voice.

I looked at her. I reached out and cupped and fondled her big breasts.

She didn't stop me. But she said again, "Please leave."

I shrugged and got up. Her eyes were on my big cock as I pulled on my pants.

When I was about to leave, she said "You won't tell anyone, right?" She had a desperate, panicked look in her face.

"I promise," I said. And I meant it. Fucking Suzanne had been better than I ever imagined, but I had no intention of burning her with Fred. I'm not that much of a dick.

CHAPTER 2

My family lived in a small beach town. As soon as I got old enough, I began waiting tables at an oceanside restaurant. The restaurant was on the boardwalk so it was very popular with tourists. It was popular with locals too, because the owner/chef always served fresh fish caught that day by local fishermen, and it had creative cocktails and an affordable wine list.

People always assumed the primo job at the beach was to be a lifeguard. They figured it was a status thing, like being on the football team, or (for chicks) being a cheerleader. Maybe, but who cared about that? Waiting tables for rich tourists and thirsty locals was where the money's at.

And, I always went to the lifeguard parties anyway. It wasn't like you needed a formal invitation. I just showed up with some beer and a baggie of weed, and I was always welcomed with open arms.

You know who also crashed lifeguard parties? All the pretty tourist high school and college girls who pranced around in tiny bikinis on their once-a-year beach vacation. So I got my share of young tourist pussy.

I always stayed away from local girls. The last thing I wanted was a pissed off father or big brother coming after me with a baseball bat. Fucking Suzanne was an exception, and a one-time thing. I'm pretty sure I could take Fred, as I'm bigger. But who wants that hassle?

Still, I thought about that night with Suzanne a lot. On a hotness scale, she doesn't score very high. I mean, her face was cute, and her big tits were something. And I liked her bare pussy. But any one of those young tourist chicks was sexier than Suzanne.

What got me charged up was fucking Fred's girlfriend. Taking a chick who belonged to another dude. That's what I thought about, and I admit, jerked off to more than a few times.

It was Christmas break and I was working a few shifts to make some spending money for college. A group of 8 ladies came in. They were locals and regulars at my restaurant. They dined and drank (mostly drank) at the restaurant about once a month for their ladies night.

Here's some inside baseball about restaurants. The best-looking waitress gets assigned to men-only tables, and the best-looking waiter gets assigned to women-only tables. That way the tips are higher, and since we share tips, everyone's good with this setup.

I was the best-looking guy, so I got assigned to the ladies' table. I recognized their faces but didn't know their names. Their kids were younger, kindergarten and first grade thereabouts, so it wasn't like they were moms of any of my friends.

I knew from experience that these MILFs got touchy-feely after a few cocktails and bottles of wine. If they flirted with me, I flirted back. If they grabbed my ass, I grinned at the ass-grabber. That was how you got a good tip.

Anyway, the MILFs left a good tip and that would have been the end of it. But when I went outside at the end of my shift, I saw one of the MILFs leaning against her car and looking upset. It was clear to me immediately what was going on. After her friends left, her car broke down.

"You okay?" I asked.

"My car broke down and it takes hours for a tow truck to show up," she said annoyed.

"The beach," I lamented.

"Yeah," she agreed. That was how it was in a resort town. Locals weren't the hardest working people. I was as bad as everyone else. I wasn't the smartest guy in the world, and not very motivated. That was beach life. Locals were just as likely to hit the beach and surf if the waves were good, than go to work.

"You need a ride home?" I asked.

"Could you?" she said looking grateful. "My husband took the kids camping this weekend. Otherwise he would've picked me up already."

As we drove, she told me her name was Molly, and I told her my name. Clark.

I remembered her at the restaurant. Not just their girls' nights, but with her family. I remembered she had two young boys. Maybe 6 and 9? I was bad trying to guess the ages of young kids.

Molly was clearly tipsy, so she didn't notice as I glanced over and checked her out. She was attractive. *Very* attractive. Mid 30s, but she could pass for a twenty-something. Blonde hair down to her shoulders. Pretty, innocent face. An amazing smile with perfect white teeth. Slim with a small bust. First class legs. Long and shapely.

I thought about Suzanne, and how I'd gotten her to cheat on Fred. Could I possibly get Molly to cheat on her husband? The idea got me hot.

Earlier, I'd noticed Molly checking me out in the restaurant. She didn't grab my ass the way some of her friends did, but she flirted with me, even doing a hair flip when I was taking her order.

She no doubt thought it was harmless flirting with a boy over 15 years younger. What would she do if I seriously hit on her? Would she stay faithful to her husband? Suddenly I wanted to know.

As we drove, we continued flirting. Nothing over the top, but I kept her laughing, and a couple of times she playfully punched my arm.

"So Clark – is that a family name?" Molly asked. "Because whenever I hear Clark, I think Clark Kent."

"I like to think I'm named after Superman's secret identity," I said with a grin at her.

Molly laughed. "So do you have superpowers?" she asked with a grin back at me.

"Yes I do," I told her. "I'd show you want they are, but then your husband would probably want to Kryptonite my ass."

That's when Molly laughed and punched my arm.

As we approached her house, I was trying to figure out moves to get into her pants. But then I got a lucky break. In her tipsy state, she took an awkward step out of my car and turned her ankle. She couldn't walk so I ended up carrying her into her house. It was like the groom carrying his new bride over the threshold. The image made my cock jerk in my pants.

"Wow, you're really strong," she admired as I gently laid her on the sofa. Molly had a slim figure, but she was tall for a girl (maybe 5 feet 7 or so), so I could see how some dudes – like her husband – might find it hard to carry her because of leverage. But I'm well over 6 feet and still had my linebacker and power forward body from high school, so for me it was no problem.

"You're light as a feather," I said grinning at her.

Molly was clearly pleased with the compliment. "You can stop Clark," she said with a laugh. "You've already got your tip."

"No, seriously, I can tell you're in good shape," I said.

"I do Pilates four times a week," she said proudly.

"Awesome. That's great core work," I said.

"You do Pilates?" she asked, clearly interested to talk to someone about her favorite exercise routine.

"I'm more of a yoga guy," I said grinning.

"Oh you're full of shit," she said with a laugh.

"No, really," I said. Moving a little into her personal space, I gave her a teasing grin and said, "As long as it's *hot* yoga."

Molly laughed and punched my arm again. She was clearly flattered that I was flirting with her. After all, I was a good-looking guy, and probably 15 years younger than her.

"I should get some ice for that ankle," I said moving to her kitchen. I stuffed some ice in a plastic bag. Then I saw a bottle of white wine. I poured a couple glasses. I figured it would help if I kept her tipsy.

Molly laughed when she saw the wine glasses. But she readily took one of the glasses when I handed it to her, taking a sip.

I sat next to her on the sofa and put her feet onto my lap. I took off and tossed her shoes onto the floor (she was wearing black pointy toe flats). Then I gently placed the ice bag on her ankle. It didn't look bad, barely any swelling.

Then I lightly tickled the sole of her foot.

She laughed and said "Stop." I grinned and we both sipped our wines.

"You have pretty feet," I said.

She laughed and shook her head, again probably thinking this was just harmless flirting with the kid from the restaurant. She took another sip of the wine.

Then I raised the stakes. With the ice bag on one ankle, I gently caressed her other ankle.

"Are you hitting on me?" she asked, another laugh in her voice. She was clearly not taking me seriously. She didn't consider me a threat to her wedding vows.

"I think you're really hot Molly," I said, looking seriously at her as I continued to caress her ankle.

"Okay, now I know you're full of shit," she said, pulling a stray lock of her blonde hair behind her ear as she blushed. She fucking blushed. She took a big gulp of wine. Her glass was almost empty, so I poured my glass into hers. She laughed.

"You cannot think I'm hot," Molly said with the laugh still in her voice. "What are you, 19?"

"18," I said.

"God, you're so young," Molly said with half a laugh in her voice. "You're 17 years younger than me. I used to babysit boys your age. I mean, when I was younger, and you were younger. You know what I mean."

"35 huh?" I said grinning. As I continued to caress her ankle, I joked, "So you're clearly a MILF. What I don't get is, are you a cougar too? Or do you become that when you're older? But then are you a MILF and a cougar at the same time?"

Molly laughed again. It was a nervous laugh though, and her blush deepened. "I can see you've thought a lot about this," she said. With a hint of sadness, she added, "No one's ever called me a MILF before."

I moved my hand up so now I was caressing her calf just below her knee. "Your legs are amazing," I told her.

"We really can't do this Clark," she said. She pulled her legs away. "I'm not a girl you meet at a lifeguard party."

"How do you know what goes on at lifeguard parties?" I asked.

"I've lived at the beach all my life," Molly said. "I used to be a lifeguard."

"So you picked fame over fortune," I joked.

She laughed. She knew what I was talking about. "I waited tables too, just like you," she said.

"A hard-working girl," I said.

She shrugged and said, "I guess you waiter to make money for college? I did the same thing."

I looked at her and felt a connection. She was a generation older, but we'd walked the same path in life.

But I didn't want to be Molly's friend. I wanted to stick my cock into her married pussy.

"So at lifeguard parties ... you used to ...," I began. I didn't have to complete the sentence. All the locals knew. It was the same in all beach towns. With all the drinking and partying, it was common for the lifeguards to hook up.

"No, I didn't party a lot," Molly said. "Like I said, I had two jobs. And I was already dating Johnny then. We were high school sweethearts."

"Johnny," I thought. That was her husband. I liked knowing his name. I wondered what Johnny would think if he knew his wife was getting hit on by a guy half her age?

"So maybe you need to make up for lost time," I joked. I moved my hand back onto her knee.

Molly laughed. She pushed my hand away. "Clark, look, you're sweet," she said. "But I'm married. Happily married. And I have 2 kids."

"But they're away, right?" I said. "For the weekend."

Molly stared at me. She was finally getting it. I wasn't playing. I was serious about getting into her pants.

"This isn't going to happen Clark," she said, shaking her head.

I shifted on the sofa so I was sideways to her. "Molly you're really hot," I said. I took her hand and put it onto my crotch over my pants. "Look what you've done to me."

Molly's eyes went wide as she felt my erection. And my size. Clearly I was bigger than Johnny-boy.

Before she could react, I leaned in and kissed her. She probably expected my kisses to be those of an inexperienced 18 year old. But I'd had a lot of practice.

I kissed her tenderly and soft, going slow, not rushing it. She tried to pull away, but I put my hand behind her head. I was gentle but persistent. Eventually, she parted her lips and I slowly pushed my tongue in. As I kissed her, I swirled my tongue over hers. Her tongue was very soft.

Eventually Molly began kissing me back. I kissed her more urgently. She began pressing her tongue against mine. Tentatively at first, but then more passionately.

After minutes of kissing, I pulled back and looked at her. Her pretty face was flushed and she was breathing hard. She looked confused. Unsure what was happening. I leaned in and kissed her again.

After more minutes of kissing, I trailed my lips down to her neck. I began kissing her neck below her ear. She groaned "Oh god …."

After kissing and sucking her neck for long moments, I returned to kissing her lips. I moved my hands to her breasts. I fondled her tits over her blouse and bra.

"Clark we can't," she protested. I pulled her blouse from her skirt. I moved my hands under her blouse, pushing it up. I also pushed up her bra. I was kissing her again as I cupped her naked breasts.

"Clark we can't," she said again, but this time her protests were muffled since my lips were covering hers. I fondled her breasts and rubbed her nipples with my thumbs. Molly moaned into my mouth "Oh god ...."

I felt like Molly was ripe for the taking. So I quickly lowered myself to the floor, onto my knees. I pushed her skirt up until it was around her waist. I saw a wet spot in her panties. I quickly curled a finger into the gusset and pulled it aside, revealing her pussy. I saw she kept herself nicely trimmed. Then I lowered my head and began eating her.

Molly grabbed at the cushions and moaned as I feasted on her pussy. "I can't believe this is happening," she between between moans.

She probably thought I'd get her off with my tongue, and then she'd jerk me off with her hand, and that would be it. Technically cheating, but not that bad. Maybe she'd even giggle about it conspiratorially with her girlfriends at their next ladies' night.

But I wasn't going to settle for a hand job. As I ate her, I pulled my pants down, freeing my hard cock. She couldn't see me doing this since I was kneeling on the floor. I'd pulled this move many times with girls.

When I sensed she was close to cumming, I quickly rose up. With my arms under her knees, I pulled her towards me so her ass was almost off the sofa. Then, guiding my hard cock with my hand, I pressed my cockhead between her pussy lips, and pushed into her.

"Oh god no!" Molly squealed with alarm as she felt my cock penetrate her.

"Pull out! Put out!" she pleaded, but of course I didn't.

I pushed more of my man meat into her. "Oh god it's too big! It hurts!" Molly said, tears welling up in her eyes.

"I'll be gentle," I promised as I shoved more of my cock into her.

When I was balls deep, I stopped moving to let her get used to my size. I reached out and cupped her breasts. They were small but went well with her slim petite body. I fondled her breasts and thumbed her nipples.

"Please we can't be doing this," Molly said. She looked scared and panicked, but also aroused. "I'm married. Johnny ...."

"He'll never know," I promised. "I'll never tell anyone." Then I began moving in and out of her pussy. I was fucking her. I was fucking her married pussy.

"Oh god!" Molly lamented as she realized she was getting fucked. As she realized she was cheating on her husband.

As I slowly fucked her, I crossed my arms and pulled my shirt over my head.

"Wow," Molly softly moaned as she looked at my chest. I was 18 years old and worked out all the time with free weights. My chest and arms were hard, muscled and well defined. I had what the locals called a "beach body." And I'd seen her husband – Johnny – on the beach a couple of times, in his bathing suit with his t-shirt off. I remembered he was thin with little muscular definition, no doubt a desk jockey who didn't invest much time or effort on his body. He was paying for it now as his wife gazed lustfully at my ripped chest.

I took her hands and brought them up to my chest. She flinched like she'd just touched a hot stove. But I held her hands tight against my chest, and soon she was running her hands over my pecs and abs.

"Your hands feel really good Molly. They're really soft," I told her as I stared down into her face. "Your pussy feels really good. It's soft too."

"You didn't pull on a condom," she said worriedly.

"No," I said. "I don't have one." I was lying. I always kept a condom in my wallet. But I wanted to fuck her bareback. And I figured she was safe since she was married.

"Don't worry. I get tested regularly," I told her. That was true. I fucked too many girls not to get tested regularly.

"You still have to pull out," she said pleadingly.

"I will," I promised. Then I leaned down and kissed her as I began fucking her faster and harder.

I put her slim, sexy legs on my shoulders and leaned towards her so her thighs pressed against her tits. Then I started to really pound her.

"Oh god oh god oh god ...," she moaned over and over again. Probably it had been years since she'd been fucked so hard. Or maybe Johnny-boy had never fucked her hard.

Then she squeezed her eyes shut and rolled her head back as she screamed, "Oh shit! Shit! Shit! Oh god!"

I felt her pussy spasming on my cock. She was cumming. I'd just made the married bitch cum on my cock.

I wanted to kiss her. I liked kissing a girl when she was cumming on my cock. But instead I looked at her face. Damn. Molly was so pretty when she came. Wow. The sight of her face when she was cumming practically took my breath away.

"Please stop, stop," Molly said, her body still spasming. "Give me a second," she panted.

I stopped moving with my cock still buried deep inside her. She was breathing hard as she looked up at me. She looked surprised and confused, and also a bit awed. Like she couldn't believe what I'd just done to her.

"Did that feel good?" I asked her.

After a moment, she hesitantly nodded her pretty head yes.

I leaned down and kissed her. She didn't resist or hesitate at all this time. She kissed me back, even wrapping her arms around my neck. As we made out, I ran my hands over her petite, tight body, touching and caressing her everywhere. I felt her moan into my mouth.

I began moving in and out again. I started slow but soon was fucking her hard and fast. At one point, I flipped her over so she was on her hands and knees. Then I began to really ram her. She grunted "ah ah ah ah" as I pounded her, with her head buried in the pillow and her fingers clutching the sofa cushions.

After long minutes of hard fucking, I felt her body tense and she arched her head back. Her face was strained and her lips parted, and she cried out "ohhhhh goddddd!" She was about to cum again.

I twisted her slightly so her face was somewhat turned to me. I planted my lips over hers as Molly's body spasmed with her orgasm. I kept kissing her through her orgasm, and I felt her heavy breaths as she moaned into my mouth.

I was ready to cum. I twisted her more, so now she was on her back again. With my lips still planted over hers, I pounded hard once, twice, three times, each time shooting my seed into her married pussy. This time it was Molly who felt my moans and grunts in her mouth.

I pulled out and sat up. There wasn't enough room on the sofa to lie beside her. That's okay. I liked looking at her as she was panting. Fuck, she had a nice body. For a 35 year old, and despite giving birth two times, her body was tight and her stomach flat and taut. Her tits were little, but that was okay with me. I liked flat chested girls.

Molly got up on her elbows and looked at my crotch. She saw the white cream covering my softening cock. Then her hand shot to her pussy. She felt the wetness there. "Oh god you came inside me," she said panicked. "You promised to pull out."

"Sorry, I forgot," I said, still breathing hard. I was lying of course. I wanted to shoot my load in the married bitch. I wondered if she was on birth control. The possibility that she wasn't sent deliciously tingles down my spine and to my cock.

"Fuck," Molly sighed, and she fell back onto the sofa. "You need to go Clark."

I reached out and cupped one of her breasts. I gently fondled it and thumbed the nipple. "We can go again," I said. "Give me a minute. I'll be hard again."

Molly stared at me. Did she look ... tempted?

"You really need to go Clark," she finally said. She looked away, not able to look into my face.

I was still fondling her tit. I decided to be a dick. I grinned and said, "You ever cum that hard with Johnny? And twice, so fast?" I flicked the flat of my thumb over her nipple and I felt her flinch.

Molly sat up and pushed my hand away. She scowled at me. From somewhere she grabbed a blanket and covered herself. "Go Clark," she said. "Please."

I scoffed as I got up and dressed. As I was about to leave, Molly said, "You promise you won't tell anyone?"

I looked at her. Then I grinned and said, "Let me see your sexy MILF body one more time."

Molly hesitated, then pulled the blanket open. I stared at her body for long moments. Then I said, "I promise." A few moments later I was in my car, driving home, with a big grin on my face.

I'd done it. Just like with Suzanne. I'd gotten Molly to cheat on her husband.

CHAPTER 3

It was spring break, but I had to stay at school to finish a term paper. Life sucked because I was pretty much alone in an empty campus.

One day after working all day in the library, I went to the bar at the Marriott next to the airport. I knew business people stayed at his Marriott before flying home the next morning.

I was beginning to realize I got off on fucking girls who belonged to other men. I got my share of college pussy, and tourist pussy when I was back home, but the extra spice of fucking another man's property really got me going. I thought about what happened with Suzanne and Molly all the time, and often when my dick was in another girl, I fantasized about those experiences.

So I went to the airport Marriott hunting for married girls. I wanted to stick my dick into one of them and get her to cheat on her husband.

I settled in at the bar and used my fake ID to get a beer. I didn't look 21, but as long as you had an ID, most bartenders served you. They were like me, always after tips.

I looked around at the crowd, checking out if there were any pretty girls wearing wedding rings. Then I was shocked to see Fred and Suzanne sitting over in a corner. They were holding hands, and they didn't look happy. What the hell? Were they breaking up?

I picked up my beer and walked over. "Hey guys, what the fuck are you doing here?" I asked with a grin. "Long time no see buddy," I said, shaking Fred's hand.

"Fred got picked for a big Peace Corp job," Suzanne said. "He's flying out tonight. He'll be gone a year."

"Oh, wow. That's really great man," I said. I knew Fred was one of those idealistic *save the world* dudes. They were both happy about his new gig, but sad they'd be apart a year.

I knew they wanted to be alone before his flight, so I quickly said goodbye and left the bar. I couldn't exactly hit on a married chick with Fred and Suzanne there so I went home.

That night in bed, I looked up at the ceiling for a long time. I thought about that night with Suzanne. And I thought about how she was going to be alone for a year.

Eventually I pulled out my dick and jerked off.

———◉———

I waited two months. I figured that was long enough for Suzanne to get horny enough to cheat (again) on Fred.

I found her in the labs in the chem building. I knew she was there all the time, because she was pre-med (I guess I forgot to mention that Suzanne, like Fred, was super smart).

Suzanne looked warily at me as I approached. "What are you doing here?" she asked guardedly.

"Why the heck are you here at midnight Suzanne?" I asked.

"Why are you here?" she shot back. Okay, she got me there. All I could do was smile.

"So how's Fred?" I asked.

"He's good," she answered.

"You still call each other every night?" I asked.

Suzanne shook her head. "He's in Africa," she said. "Barely any cell coverage. He's got a sat phone but it's really expensive."

"Kinda wild what happened, that time we were together, and he called," I said with a grin.

"Can we not talk about it?" Suzanne said irritably.

"You tell Fred?" I asked.

"Tell him what?"

"About that night," I said.

Suzanne's eyes went wide. "Of course I didn't tell him," she said. "Are you freaking crazy?"

"I just thought you might want to get it off your chest," I said as I stared at her big bust.

Seeing where I was looking, she said "You know, my face is up here."

I grinned at her. "I bet you have to tell a lot of guys that," I said.

She scoffed, but it sounded like a laugh. "So why are you here exactly?" she asked again.

"I thought we ought to talk about that night," I said. "Clear the air."

"There's nothing to talk about," Suzanne said dismissively. "It was a mistake. It'll never happen again."

"Okay, well, that's cool," I said. "I just wanted to tell you, that I probably didn't pay that much attention to you in high school, because you were always with Fred. But I think about that night a lot. I think about you a lot. I see you differently now."

I guess I need to give you some backstory. Back in high school, I ran in the same social circles as Fred and Suzanne. But we were on opposite ends of popularity, with me at the top and Fred and Suzanne towards the bottom. They were honor students. I was on the football and basketball teams.

They were class officers. I was invited to be on the prom court (I declined because who the fuck wants to help decorate the gym for the prom?).

They were a couple all through high schools. I went through a bunch of girlfriends, including the senior prom queen (when I was a sophomore), a college sorority chick (when I was a junior), and a number of very pretty cheerleaders (from my school and a couple of our rivals).

So for me to tell Suzanne I thought about her a lot, she was certain to be interested, and flattered too.

She confirmed it when she smiled shyly, and asked "You think about me? How am I different?"

"You're really pretty," I said. I was laying it on really thick. But forgive me, I was trying to get into her pants.

"I mean, you've always been pretty," I said. "I guess I never thought about you that way since you were always with Fred. And you're sexy. You've got a really nice body."

Suzanne blushed and said, "We shouldn't be talking about this."

"Why not?"

"You know why not," she said. "I'm with Fred."

"At least now you've been with someone besides Fred," I said. I knew she gave her virginity to Fred, and had not been with anyone else.

Except me.

Suzanne was really blushing now. "Why exactly are you here?" she asked.

"Have I ever played the wrist game with you?" I asked.

"What?" she said, confused by the non-sequitur.

"I've always been fascinated by wrists," I said. "I have no idea why. But do you know there are 8 bones in the wrist?"

"Yeah, I mean, I'm pre-med," Suzanne said with a *hello?* tone of voice.

"Yeah right," I said with a friendly laugh. "Okay, show me your wrists."

"What? Why?"

"Come on, put your wrists on the table," I said in a playful voice. I took her hands and turned them palms up so the underside of her wrists were exposed.

"Okay, this is the wrist game," I said grinning at her. "I tickle your wrists, and we see how long you can take it before you pull your wrists away. The record is 23 seconds."

"This is stupid," Suzanne said.

"That's because I'm stupid," I said with a laugh. "I'm not a Brainiac like you and Fred."

A quick interlude here. I was bringing up Fred on purpose. I wanted into Suzanne's pants, but I didn't want her to forget about Fred. I wanted her to give herself to me *even though* she was thinking about her boyfriend. *That* would be a serious conquest. A serious fuck you to Freddy-boy.

Suzanne shook her head like I was an idiot. But she was smiling slightly. She was used to being around Fred, who was smart and mature. I'd been called a lot of things, but never *smart* or *mature*. So she probably thought I was a harmless idiot. But like that night with Molly, she didn't realize the danger she was in.

I began tracing light circles on her wrists with my fingertips. She immediately pulled her hands away. "This is stupid," she said, scratching her wrists.

"Come on, try to get to at least 10 seconds," I said. She frowned and reluctantly put her hands back down.

I traced lines and circles on her wrists again. She was grimacing but made it to 10 seconds.

"See, you did it," I said. Before she could pull her hands away, I scratched her wrists for her. Then I began to lightly caress her wrists with the flats of my thumbs. I wasn't tickling her anymore. I was caressing her.

Suzanne flushed, her cheeks going red. "Clark you should stop," she said.

I leaned over and kissed her. She pulled away. I kissed her again, this time putting my hand behind her head. She tried to pull away but I was persistent, pushing my tongue into her mouth. Eventually I felt Suzanne giving in and kissing me back.

As we sucked face, I moved my hand to her breasts. I was looking forward to seeing and playing with her double Ds again.

Suzanne pulled away from my lips. Breathing hard, she said, "Clark, no, we can't do this here," she panted. "Someone might come in."

It was after midnight and I couldn't imagine anyone coming into the lab this late. But you never knew with geeks.

I scanned the room. I saw a door with one of those thin vertical windows. A breakroom?

I didn't care what it was. All that mattered was it was there.

I dragged Suzanne into the room and locked the door. Before she could complain, I took off my shirt and hung it over the door.

When I turned back, Suzanne was looking at my chest. She had a hungry look in her face.

As she stared at my muscles, she said "I used to look at you on the beach."

I pulled her hands to my chest, to my well-defined pecs. "You ever fantasize about me while Fred is fucking you?" I asked with a mischievous grin.

"Fred and I don't fuck," she said. "We make love."

I laughed. *Okay, whatever*, I thought.

I pushed Suzanne down onto her knees. Then I quickly freed my cock. Last time Suzanne didn't suck me. This time she would.

I wanted to see my cock in the mouth of Fred's girlfriend.

"You suck Fred when you make love?" I asked as I pressed the big cockhead of my dick against her lips.

"Sometimes," she said.

I rubbed my cockhead all over her face. "Fred ever do this to you?" I asked.

"No," Suzanne said. "He's a gentleman."

I laughed again. Then I said "Open your mouth Suzanne."

She parted her lips, and I pushed my cockhead against them.

"You'll have to open wider," I told her.

She opened her mouth as wide as possible. Still, she struggled to take my cock into her mouth. She wasn't very good at giving head. Or at least, not with a cock as big as mine.

"Look up at me," I said. She looked up at me with her pretty brown eyes. God this was hot! I didn't care how good she was at oral. All that mattered was my cock was in her mouth! Fred's girlfriend's mouth!

"Ah yeah Suzanne, you're good at this," I lied. "Fred's a lucky boy."

"Take off your blouse while you blow me. Let me see those big tits," I told her. With only a couple of inches in her mouth, she reached down and unbuttoned her blouse, and took it off. Then she reached behind her and unsnapped her bra. A moment later, the bra was on the floor next to her blouse.

I reached down and cupped and fondled her big breasts while she licked and sucked me. I knew how she liked to be touched after the last time, so soon her face was flushed and she was breathing hard. She was practically moaning on my cock as she licked and sucked it.

Enough of foreplay. I pulled her up and laid her on the sofa. I quickly pulled down her jeans, taking her panties off at the same time.

"I really like how you keep this bare," I said as I thumbed her hairless mound.

Suzanne groaned and arched her back up to press against my hand. I grinned and said "You little slut. You really need fucked, don't you?"

"Don't talk to me that way," she said. I grinned at her.

I rubbed my cock up and down her slit. "Next time I'll go down on you," I promised. "I'll make you cum on my tongue."

Her eyes fluttered as I stroked her slit with my cock. "There won't be a next time," she insisted.

I pushed my cock into her. She groaned at the penetration.

"You're so tight," I said as I strained to push my cock into her. Her face was tense too, as I stretched and filled her up. "Not used to my size, huh? I've seen Fred in the shower after PE. He's got a little dick. No wonder your pussy's so tight."

"Please don't talk about him," Suzanne said, her face strained as I pushed more of my fat cock into her.

I grinned at her. I liked talking about Fred as I fucked his girlfriend. As she cheated on him. It was fucking hot.

I leaned down and kissed her. She turned her head away. "Just fuck me," she said. "I don't want you to kiss me."

"We were kissing already in the lab," I reminded her.

"Clark ... I need to keep something for Fred," she said. There was regret and sadness in her voice and face, but she wasn't telling me to pull out. The horny bitch needed fucked.

"It doesn't work that way Suz," I said. I took her hands and pulled them above her head. Then I slammed the rest of my cock inside her. As she grunted at the penetration, I planted my lips over hers. She resisted for a few seconds, but then she was kissing me back. We traded spit for long moments, our tongues dancing.

While still kissing, I began moving in and out. As I fucked her, I moved my hands to her breasts. I roughly fondled her big tit meat and rubbed her nipples hard.

"Oh god!" she moaned, rolling her head back so our lips parted.

"Your pussy feels good Suz," I said to her as I moved in and out of her canal. "You like my cock inside you?"

"Yeah, yeah, yeah ...," she said, moaning out the words.

I fucked her harder and faster, and she was panting into my face. "Oh fuck!" she cried, and I felt her body tense. She rolled her head back and her lips parted, and she stayed that way for a moment, like she was at the top of a wave. Then the wave crashed down and she came.

"Oh god!" she cried as orgasmic pleasure slammed her body. I felt her pussy walls squeeze around my cock as I fucked her through her orgasm.

"Give me a second," she panted, needing a moment to recover.

"No way, I'm close," I told her as I kept pounding her pussy.

"You put on a condom, right?" she asked.

"No."

Her eyes went wide. "You need to pull out Clark!" she said, panic in her voice.

"Do you make Fred wear condoms?" I asked as I continued fucking her.

"He always wears condoms," she said. "We have things we want to do in life. We don't want kids yet."

"You're not on the pill?" I asked, by eyes going wide with surprise.

Suzanne shook her head. "You have to pull out Clark!" she said urgently.

"Oh god Suzanne! You dirty girl!" I moaned. The bitch wasn't on birth control! She was unprotected!

I leaned down and kissed her again as I pounded away on her pussy. A moment later I was cumming. I didn't pull out. I knew it was a dick move, but I couldn't help myself. I was fucking Fred's girlfriend. I was giving her the best sex of her life. Now I might be getting her pregnant. It was the best orgasm of my life!

The next day, I went with Suzanne to the CVS. She had never taken a morning after pill before. She'd never needed it. Fred was a good guy, and always wore condoms.

I was there for emotional support. Suzanne equated morning after pills with abortion, and she was a pro-life girl. Taking a morning after pill was a moral defeat for her. But she couldn't risk it. Fred had been gone over two months, and if she got pregnant ....

Well, Fred was a smart guy. He could count.

So Suzanne was upset. Distraught even. That's why I was there, a person to lean on. Even though she hated me. But it's not like she could ask any of her other friends to come with her.

Suzanne went up to the pharmacist alone of course, while I pretended to shop a few aisles away. She didn't want anyone to see us together, especially while buying a morning after pill.

As I watched her talk to the pharmacist, I felt regret. I felt like an asshole, a dick.

But I knew I'd be fucking Fred's girlfriend again. And it would be even easier next time. I'd seen it with other girls. Suzanne had gotten a taste of my dick, and she'd want more.

CHAPTER 4

I was starting to get to know myself. About my new kink, that is.

I got off on fucking other men's girls. But it was more than that.

I wanted to fuck a girl better than her husband (or boyfriend) ever had. I wanted to see that awed look in her face that said *"what did you just do to me?"*

And I got off on talking about her husband (boyfriend) as she was cheating on him.

I found myself not as interested in single girls. At parties, I was drawn to girls with boyfriends. Around town, like in bars, I looked for girls wearing wedding rings.

I had to be careful though. I didn't want a jealous husband coming after me with a baseball bat (or worse). And getting a married girl alone to make my moves wasn't easy. What happen with Molly was sort of a one-off. She got a flat tire, and her husband and kids were away for the weekend. How often was that gonna happen?

I also wanted to stay away from local girls in my hometown. I didn't want to get a reputation where I lived for being – what would you call me? A predator of married girls?

A hunter of girls who belonged to other men?

I went to the airport hotel a couple of times, hunting for married chicks. But both times I didn't see anyone interesting.

Then it was almost summer and exam time. I hated studying and mostly watched NBA playoffs. I was on the verge of flunking out. I was beginning to question whether college was for me. I wasn't book smart. And what was the point of spending tons of money on tuition if I'd end up waiting tables anyway? Also, I hated going to class. The best things about college were the parties and girls, but I could get that back home.

Anyway, I managed to pass all my classes (just barely) and decided to wait until the end of summer to figure out if I wanted to go back to college.

It was my last night in the dorm and I was packing up. Almost everyone had already left so the dorm was mostly empty.

There was a knock and I opened the door. Standing there was Suzanne.

She came in and I closed the door.

"You want a beer?" I asked.

"Sure."

I had a couple left in the frig. I opened them and we clicked bottles. "To the end of our freshman year," I said.

"Yeah," she said.

"You get good grades?" I asked. "Straight As?"

"Are you making fun of me?" she asked.

"No. I think it's cool you're so smart," I said. I was being honest. I wish I was as smart as her. Or even half as smart as her.

"How'd you do?" she asked.

I shrugged and smiled sheepishly. "Not straight As," I said with a laugh. She gave me a kind understanding smile. She knew I wasn't the brightest light in the room.

"How's Fred?" I asked.

"He's good."

"You two still together?"

"Of course we're still together," Suzanne snapped. "Why would you ask that?"

"I don't know," I said. "Long distance relationships are tough. And you're here."

Suzanne stared into my face for long moments. Then she said in a soft voice, "I'm on the pill now."

I stared back into her face. Then I said, "Take off your blouse Suzy."

"Don't call me that," she said.

"Why?"

"Fred calls me that," Suzanne said. I knew that of course. I wanted to hear her say it. It got me hot.

"Take off your blouse Suzy," I said again.

She sighed, realizing I was in control, not her. She began unbuttoning her blouse.

When it was off, I said "Now the bra."

She reached back and unsnapped her bra. Then she let it fall off her arms.

I stared at her big tits. They really were nice. Big and perfectly shaped. They sagged a little, no one would call them perky. But they got me hard looking at them.

"What's your bra size?" I asked.

Suzanne flushed. "Why does it matter?" she asked, trying to maintain her dignity.

"Just curious," I said with a shrug. "Does Fred know?"

"Of course he knows," she said impatiently. "Sometimes he buys me lingerie."

"Like for Valentine's day?" I asked.

Suzanne was getting mad because I was talking about her boyfriend so much. "This was a bad idea," she said annoyed, reaching for her bra and blouse to put them back on.

"It's okay, Suzy, chill," I said as I moved towards her. I pulled her towards me and kissed her. Soon we were passionately kissing. I ran my hands over her body, especially her tits. I knew how she liked to be touched, so in moments she was moaning into my mouth.

I pushed her down onto her knees. "Suck me off," I told her.

"Last time you said you'd go down on me," Suzanne said testily. She was a smart, strong girl. She wanted to maintain her dignity and keep some control over what was happening.

That wasn't going to work with me. Maybe that's how it worked with Fred, but not me. I was in control, not her. I needed her to understand that.

"Suck me off Suz, and then you'll get your turn," I told her as I pulled my cock from my pants. My thick meat was half hard. "Lick me and get me hard," I told her.

Suzanne glared at me for a moment. Then she extended her tongue and began licking my cock.

"You shaved," she said between licks.

"Yeah. Now I'm bare like you," I said. She glared at me again but I sensed a smile there too.

Recently I'd begun shaving off my pubic hair. I bought this shaver called the *Lawn Mower* and it made manscaping quick. That, plus some hair removal lotion, and I was hairless around my cock and down my crack. A man's Brazilian. I figured, if I was hunting after girls who belonged to other men, I wanted to look the part. I wanted to look like a porn star.

I pulled up my shaft and said, "Lick my balls, Suz." Suzanne did as I asked. I could tell she was getting hot from working on my big cock.

"Yeah, suck them, yeah," I moaned, enjoying how she was swallowing my balls. I was fully hard now.

I took my cock in my hand and pressed the big cockhead against her cheek. I thought about all the times in high school I'd seen Suzanne and Fred together, holding hands, snuggling, kissing, doing all the romantic things couples in love do. And now my big dick was pressed against her cheek.

It got me fucking hot!

"Suck me off and make me cum with your mouth," I told her, pressing the cockhead against her lips. "Then I'll get you off with my tongue."

She hesitated, and I said, "Don't worry. I'll fuck you too. We're going to be together all night, Suzy."

"I'm not sleeping with you," she said.

I grinned and said "Who said anything about sleep?"

I reached down and squeezed one of her big tits. "You fuck anyone since going on the pill?" I asked as I fondled her breast.

"Are you crazy?" she asked scornfully. If she had, it meant she had cheated on Fred. It seemed I was the only guy she was unfaithful with.

I laughed. "So you're on the pill now," I said. "I can cum in your pussy as much as I want."

"Are you safe?" she asked me.

"I get tested all the time," I assured her. With a laugh, I added, "There are lots of horny girls like you who are sluts for my big cock."

"You're a pig," she said, moving to get up and leave.

I pushed her down on her knees again. With a laugh, I said, "Oh come on Suzy. I'm just shitting with you. You know I think you're super smart. I just told you that. You're gonna go way farther in life than me. Fred will too. You think I don't know that?"

My humble admission seemed to calm her. She settled back on her knees with my hard cock pointing at her face.

"So what are you going to tell Fred? About going on the pill?"

She'd already thought about this. "I'll tell him he doesn't have to use condoms anymore," she said.

My hard cock jerked at her words. Fred had never been inside her bareback. He'd never felt her skin-to-skin. I had. I was the first man to shoot his seed into her fertile, unprotected womb.

That realization got me fucking hot!

"Suck me off Suzy," I insisted, pressing my fat cockhead against her lips. Finally she opened her mouth wide and took me in.

Suzy wasn't used to my size and could only take a couple inches into her mouth. She mostly licked and sucked while using her hands to stroke me.

But seeing my cock in the mouth of Fred's girlfriend really got me going. I felt my orgasm building.

"I'm cumming," I moaned. Suzanne tried to pull away but I held her head tight. "Swallow it," I told her.

Moments later I was cumming and ejaculating into her mouth. With my hands tightly holding the back of her head, she had no choice but to swallow it all. I saw her throat muscles working overtime to handle my large load.

Suzanne gasped when I finally let her head go and she pulled off my cock. As she panted for air, I rubbed my cockhead over her face, painting her sweet face with the remains of my cum and her spit coating my cock.

"You're disgusting," she said scornfully.

"Fred doesn't do this to you?" I said as I continued to rub my cockhead across her cute face.

"No. Fred's a nice man," Suzanne said.

"Fred's not a man. He's a boy," I told her. I was getting off on demeaning her boyfriend. The fact that he was my friend wasn't stopping me. "You're learning what it's like to be with a man."

I picked her up and put her on the sofa, on her back. I quickly tugged off her shoes, socks, jeans and panties. I thumbed her bare mound. "I want you to grow some hair here," I told her. "A thin landing strip."

"Fred likes me the way I am," Suzanne said.

"And where are you gonna get dick for the next year?" I asked her.

"This is the last time," she insisted.

"Come on Suzy, stop with the bullshit," I said. "This will *not* be the last time we're together. You went on the pill for me. You're a horny bitch and Freddy boy is away for a year. And maybe you think I'm an ass but you like my dick, and you know I'll keep my mouth shut. So I think you should do what I want instead of what Freddy-boy wants."

"Don't call him Freddy," Suzanne said. "He hates that."

I grinned at her. This was so much fun, and so fucking hot!

I opened Suzanne's legs and went down on her. I used all my tricks on her pussy and clit. I wanted this to be the best oral of her life. By the time I was done with her, she wouldn't care if I called her boyfriend "Freddy-dumb-shit" or "Little-dick-Freddy."

Soon she was writhing under my tongue. She grabbed my hair and tugged me closer to her pussy, moaning, "Oh god, oh god, don't stop Clark, don't stop ...."

When she came, her chubby legs slammed down onto my back as her body convulsed with an explosion of orgasmic pleasure.

I gave her a few moments to catch her breath. Then I grinned and said, "Was it worth the wait?"

"Stop being such a jerk and fuck me," Suzanne said.

"I'll fuck you, don't worry about that," I said. "But I want to do something else first."

I stuck 2 fingers into her pussy. She was soaking so when I pulled out my fingers they were wet. I coated my cock with that lubricate then moved up her body. I positioned my cock between her big breasts and pushed them together. Then I began moving back and forth.

"Freddy like fucking your big tits, Suzy?" I asked her. I could tell from her face the answer was yes.

"I bet it feels different getting your tits fucked by a big dick," I said. I was thumbing her nipples as I tit fucked her, and her face was getting flushed from growing arousal. "You know, a man's dick. Instead of Freddy's little boy dick."

"I gotta admit, your tits feel almost as good as your pussy," I said as I felt my climax building. I was telling the truth. Her breasts were silky smooth and soft, and as I pressed them together around my cock, they felt like a tight pussy.

Suzanne's eyes were getting heavy-lidded with arousal. She was getting off on this. She reached up and put her palms on my chest, running her fingertips along my defined pecs and abs. It was clear my muscular chest aroused her.

"Fuck I'm gonna cum," I groaned as I fucked her tits faster. Then at the last moment, I moved up and pushed my cock into her mouth. "Take it, take it, take it!" I growled as I ejaculated another load into her mouth. Like last time, I held her head so she had to swallow it.

I rolled off her. I collapsed onto my back next to her.

"Don't make me hold your head next time," I told her between pants. "Just swallow it."

She didn't say anything. She was looking up at the ceiling, occupied by her own thoughts.

I motioned to the side of the room. "There's a bathroom," I said. "Go in there and wash your face. There's probably toothpaste. Wash out your mouth. I don't want to taste cum breath when I'm kissing you. When I'm hard again I want you on top. You can fuck yourself on my cock."

Suzanne turned to look at me. She stared into my face for long moments. Then she got up and walked into the bathroom.

⸻ ❧ ⸻

We fucked, and then ordered a pizza and watched the first episode of Last of Us.

We fucked again, and at some point, fell asleep. In the middle of the night, maybe 3am or so, I woke up and fucked Suzanne again.

Then we both fell into a deep asleep.

⸻ ❧ ⸻

I woke feeling someone tugging on my arm. "Clark, wake up," I heard a voice say.

I slowly opened my eyes. My arm was around Suzanne. We'd fallen asleep spooning.

She was pushing me away. "I can't be like this with you," she said. "The sex is bad enough."

"What? Is this how you sleep with Freddy?" I asked.

"Can we stop talking about him?" Suzanne said testily as she moved to get out of my bed.

"Hold up," I said, grabbing her. "Hang out for a while. I'll get Door Dash. Coffee, donuts or something."

"Seriously? I've been here too long," she said.

"No, come on," I said. I opened the Door Dash app on my phone. She looked over my shoulder as we ordered.

"It'll be 45 minutes," I said looking at her. "What do you want to do?"

"God," Suzanne said with a laugh. She was covering herself with a blanket. I pulled it away and leaned in to kiss her.

As we kissed, I caressed her big breasts. I'd learned they were big erogenous spots for her, especially the nipples.

Soon I was on top, my cock inside her. After fucking practically constantly since yesterday, her pussy was looser, so it was easier to penetrate her. I wondered if her pussy would stay loose. What would Fred think when he got home expecting to feel his girlfriend's tight pussy hugging his thin dick, but instead finding her so loose he could barely feel anything? The thought got me so hot I was almost ready to blow.

But I forced myself not to cum. I was moving in and out really soft and slow, gently kissing and fondling her body. I wanted to show Suzanne that I could make love to her, just as good – and better – than Fred.

I wanted to show Suzanne that I was so much better than Fred, it wasn't even close. When it came to sex, he was a boy and I was a man. I wanted Suzanne to understand that. And eventually, I wanted her to admit it to me.

But I instinctively knew it would take some time before she would betray Fred that way. After all, she loved the dude, and planned to marry him. But when she did finally get there – when she said to my face "you fuck me better than Fred ever could" – *that* would be sexual conquest over another man. And that's what I wanted.

We fucked a long time, long and slow, kissing and touching each other. When she finally came, it was less intense than other times, but it seemed to go on and on until finally when it was over, she collapsed under me and her body seemed to turn to jelly and she looked like she was close to passing out.

I never stopped kissing her. Eventually, I moved up to my knees with the hard cock still deep inside her. I reached out and took both of her big tits into my hands. "What's your bra size?" I asked her.

This time she didn't resist. She said "36 DD."

"What did Fred give you for Valentine's day?"

"A red bustier," she answered.

"The next time we're together, I want you to wear it," I told her.

Suzanne stared up into my face. "I can't do that Clark," she said in a pleading voice. "Please don't ask me to do that."

"You will do it Suzy," I said, leaning back down and kissing her. "Just like you're gonna have a landing strip the next time we're together."

A moment later I came, shooting another load of my sperm into her well-used pussy.

CHAPTER 5

I moved home for summer vacation and returned to my job waiting tables at the beach front restaurant. I went to lifeguard parties and fucked a few pretty tourist girls, but my heart (and libido) wasn't really into it. What I really wanted was my next conquest of another man's girl.

Suzanne was keeping her distance and that was okay with me. Frankly I was losing interest in her. If Fred was home, it would be a different story. Like, fucking Suz before a date with Fred, so she was full of my spunk when she was with him later, now *that* would be hot. But with Fred someplace in Africa or whatever, the prospect of hooking up with Suzanne again didn't hold much appeal to me.

On Memorial Day weekend, Molly and her husband and kids came into the restaurant for dinner. Since there was a line, they waited outside on the boardwalk for a table to clear. I asked the hostess – a pretty barely legal local girl– to sit them at one of my tables. The hostess had a crush on me, so she did as I asked.

Molly was nervous when she saw I was their waiter. But I was cool about it, and by the time she finished her first vodka martini, I could tell she was feeling relaxed and enjoying dinner with her family.

As I served their entrees, I heard her husband – Johnny – complain to Molly that he still hadn't found anyone to cut their grass. I immediately said, "Don't mean to eavesdrop, but if you need someone to cut your grass, I'm available. I'm trying to make a little extra money for college."

Molly immediately shot daggers at me with her eyes, but Johnny readily agreed. We agreed on $40 per weekly cut, and I'd start the following week.

I wasn't stalking Molly, but I went by her house the days that followed to see when Johnny went to work, and when the kids were out playing. Okay, maybe I was stalking. I found out Johnny had a normal 9-5 job where he traveled to the next town, so with summer traffic, it was unlikely he'd ever come home early. The kids had a regular playdate with friends on Wednesdays, when they were gone from about mid-morning to dinner time.

So, of course I arrived the next Wednesday at 10am to cut the grass. I timed it right. When I arrived, Molly was home by herself.

"What are you doing?" she asked me. For some reason, she was whispering even though we were alone.

"I'm cutting your grass," I said.

She narrowed her eyes at me. "I have a husband and two little boys," she said. "If he finds out ...."

"Have you heard me say anything?" I asked her. "Have you heard any rumors? I said I won't say anything, and I haven't. Now can you tell me where your lawnmower is?"

She frowned at me for another moment, and then she pointed to an old shed. "In there," she said.

"Is the gas in there too?" I asked.

She shook her head. "Johnny bought a cordless electric mower. The batteries are here," she said. She got the batteries from the chargers and handed them to me.

"An electric mower? They aren't very powerful," I scoffed.

Molly shrugged. The mower was Johnny's thing, not hers.

"I guess Johnny isn't into power," I said with a grin. "He doesn't have super powers like me."

Molly narrowed her eyes at me again. My cock twitched in my pants. I was getting off on putting down the men who owned the wives I was fucking.

Then to her surprise, I abruptly took off my t-shirt right in front of her. She was looking at my ripped chest when I said, "It's hot out there."

I handed my t-shirt to her. "Can you hold onto this for me?" Without touching my t-shirt, Molly turned and walked away.

I mowed the grass. It didn't take long. Lots at the beach aren't very big. A couple times I caught Molly looking at me from the window.

As I cut the grass, I considered whether I had been too forward. But then, I decided no. Either I had a chance with Molly, or I didn't. As they say, fortune favors the brave.

When I was done, I returned to the kitchen with the 2 batteries. Molly wasn't there. There were two 20s on the table. I took them and plugged the batteries into the chargers.

The next week was the same. I mowed the grass with no shirt on. I also purposely wore low rise jeans that barely covered my ass. So my well-defined pecs and biceps, six pack abs and muscular back were all on display. I saw Molly looking at me from the window again.

I thought about Molly. She was really good looking. She was no doubt one of the prettiest girls I'd ever fucked. Even as I cut the grass, my cock got hard as I thought about fucking Molly again.

This time when I was done and returned to the kitchen with the batteries, Molly was there. She handed me two 20s.

"Thanks," I said, stuffing the money into my pocket.

Molly was looking at my chest. Then her eyes drifted lower, to my crotch. I was still hard. She saw the way my hard cock tented my pants.

"Here," she said, taking the batteries from me. She moved to put them in the chargers. But she didn't have them aligned right so they wouldn't slide in.

"Let me help," I said, moving behind her. I reached around and slid the batteries into their chargers. As I did, my bare sweaty chest pressed against her back. And my hard cock pressed against her ass.

We stayed like that for a moment, then Molly moved to the side, away from me.

"We're going to see Johnny's parents next week," she told me. "You can still cut the grass. The code to the back door lock is 0807. I'll leave the money next to the batteries."

"Is that someone's birthday?" I asked. "The code?"

Molly nodded. "It's Johnny's birthday," she said.

"Anyways, see you later," she said, turning away.

"Yeah, see you when you get back," I said as I watched her walk away. "Hey Molly."

She turned back. "What?"

"You smell really nice," I said. She did too. She smelled like roses. And baby powder.

She stared at me for a long moment. Again her eyes traveled down my chest to my crotch – lingering on the tent in my pants—and then back up to my face. Then she quicky turned away and walked deeper into her house.

The next Wednesday, I went to Molly's house early, while it was still dark. I didn't want any neighbors seeing me go into their house.

I wanted to explore Molly and Johnny's house, and I wanted to take my time doing it.

First I looked at the pictures on the walls and bookshelves. Most were of their two kids and family shots of all 4 of them. But some were of Molly and Johnny by themselves.

Molly had said they were high school sweethearts, and they definitely looked young in some of the pictures. Molly was really cute when she was a teenager. *Really cute.* She was still a looker now. But with the maturity of age, she was more pretty than cute. Even today, though, she still had that look of sweet innocence that many blue-eyed blondes have.

I focused on pictures of their wedding day. Wow. Molly looked gorgeous. Johnny was a very lucky man. He'd definitely hit way about his average in landing Molly.

I looked through the study. It looked to be Johnny's home office. There were files everywhere. I knew he was a lawyer. Clearly, the boy worked hard and he took work home.

There was a computer on the desk. I wish I knew more about computers as I'd love to see his browsing history. Did the man watch kinky porn? But I was an idiot when it came to computers so I didn't even turn it on.

I went upstairs. I didn't bother with the kids' bedrooms. I didn't care about the kids.

I went into Molly and Johnny's master bedroom. There were two closets, and it was easy to tell which one was Molly's.

I went inside and looked through her skirts, dresses and blouses. They were all sweet (like her) and nothing overly sexy. Some of the skirts and dresses were short though. Clearly, Molly knew she had nice legs and liked to show off one of her best assets.

Her shoes were stylish but, again, not overly sexy. The highest heel was maybe 2 inches.

Back in the bedroom, I looked in the side tables. No sex toys. I did find some condoms, no doubt Johnny's. They were regular size Trojans.

I looked in Molly's dresser. The top drawer held her lingerie. While the chick dressed conservatively, her lingerie was sexy. Lacy bra and panty sets, and she seemed to favor thongs.

I looked at one of the bras, to find out her bra size. 32A. I already knew she had tiny tits.

I looked at the bras more closely. Many were padded. Clearly she wanted to look bigger than she was. I wondered if she planned to get a boob job in the future. I hoped not. I liked small perky tits, and Molly's were definitely that.

On top of the lingerie was the package of Molly's birth control pills. I had a sudden inspiration.

I went back to the side tables and got one of Johnny's condoms. I put the condom next to Molly's birth control pills. Then I reached into my wallet and pulled out the condom I always kept there. My condom was a Titan 3XL. I grinned as I laid my 3XL condom next to Johnny's regular size condom.

Molly would freak when she realized I had snooped through her stuff, but she already knew I was trying to get into her pants again. And anyway, she was the one who gave me the code to her house.

I was about to leave but decided to take another pass through Molly's closet. I'd notice a box on the top shelf that appeared to be special. I took it down. It was big enough that I had to put it on the bed to open it.

I realized I hit the mother lode! Inside was Molly's wedding dress! And, laying on top of the dress was her bridal lingerie. A bra, bustier and panties, all made with delicate silk. White stockings were there too, and I knew they were the ones she wore on her wedding day because one of them was laddered. Finally, Molly's heels from that day were in the box. They were covered in ivory white fabric and had 2 inch heels, like the other shoes in her closet.

I was incredibly aroused touching Molly's wedding dress and lingerie. I went downstairs and got the wedding photo and brought it back upstairs to the master bedroom. I laid the wedding photo of Johnny and Molly on top of her wedding dress.

Then I took out my hard cock. I wrapped Molly's bridal panties around my shaft, and began jerking off. My eyes shifted back and forth between Molly in the photo and her wedding dress.

It didn't take me long to cum. Jerking my cock fast, I sprayed my cum all over their wedding photo. Most of my jism landed on Molly's face (where I aimed it), but some fell on Johnny, and that made me laugh.

After putting my cock back into my pants, I put the cum soaked wedding photo into Molly's dresser drawer, next to the condoms I'd placed there. I laid her bridal panties on top of the photo. Then I put the wedding dress box back into the closet.

As I cut the grass, I had an extra bounce in my step. Yeah, I'd gone overboard for sure, and Molly would freak when she opened her dresser drawer. But would she slap my face and fire my ass the next time she saw me, or rip off her clothes and let me fuck her brains out? I didn't know, but I'd find out next Wednesday.

CHAPTER 6

The week dragged on. And I was horny as fuck. I could easily get a young pretty tourist into my bed, but that's not what I wanted.

So I called Suzanne. "How about coming over?" I asked. "My parents are gone for the weekend. I'll get some pizza and beer and we'll binge the rest of *The Last of Us.*"

Suzanne hesitated, then said, "I don't think that's a good idea Clark."

"Why not? We had fun last time," I said.

"Because I'm with Fred. I love him. I'm going to marry him."

"And he's not here," I said. "And you're a horny slut. You love my cock. And my tongue, by the way. And by now you know I'll keep my mouth shut. Fred will never find out."

"If you're so horny, why don't you just go to a lifeguard party and hook up with a bimbo tourist?" Suzanne scoffed. She knew what lifeguard parties were like. And she knew my reputation.

"Because I don't want them," I said. "I want you. I told you. I think you're really hot. You're really pretty. Your breasts are amazing. And your pussy is really tight. You know, I think about you when I'm fucking other girls."

"You're full of shit," Suzanne said, but I could tell she was flattered. She was probably blushing like a little schoolgirl.

I *was* full of shit. I thought Suzanne was okay looking, but not *really* pretty. Her tits were big but they sagged a bit – and I knew they'd sag more as she got older. Her pussy *was* tight, but that was because Fred had a pencil dick.

But sometimes you had to lie to get what you wanted from a girl.

"I'm serious Suzy. I'm telling you the truth," I lied with my most earnest voice. "Look, we're fuck buddies. I get you're committed to Fred.

But once in your life, you should have a fuck buddy. And you're not hurting him. He'll never find out. I promise."

Suzanne was silent for long moments. I knew she was thinking through everything. The smart thing would be to stay faithful to Fred (or at least stop cheating on him) and tell me to fuck myself.

But Suzanne was a horny slut. And she liked how I fucked her.

"Okay," Suzanne finally said in a small, soft voice. "I'll come over tonight."

I grinned triumphantly! I'd done it again! Gotten a girl to cheat on the man she loved!

"Suzy ... remember what I said the last time?" I said. "The 2 things I want you to do?"

Suzanne hesitated. Then she said, in that same small soft voice, "Yes."

My grin got bigger. I felt so evil! Maybe I wasn't Superman. Maybe I was Thanos! Either way, I knew tonight would be epic!

⸻ ● ⸻

I had a pepperoni pizza and a six pack of Corona in the kitchen, but it would be a while before we got to them.

Suzanne looked pretty when she got to my house. She was wearing a dress and had makeup on. I couldn't remember the last time I saw her with makeup, if ever.

"I like that lipstick," I said. It was bright red.

"Thank you," Suzanne said kind of shyly.

"Did you buy it special for me?" I asked. "Or do you wear it for Fred too, when you want to look extra pretty?"

"Can you not talk about him?" she asked. I chuckled.

"Take off your dress Suzy," I told her.

She frowned at me. "Just like that?" she asked. Like last time, she was trying to maintain some of her dignity, and control.

"I'm not Fred," I said. "Don't expect me to act like him. So take off your dress."

Suzanne's frown deepened, but she reached behind her and unzipped her dress. Then she let it fall to the floor.

She was wearing a red bustier. Fred's gift to her last Valentine's day. White stockings were attached to the bustier's straps. It reminded me of Molly's bridal stockings. The thought made my cock throb.

"Very sexy Suzy," I said.

"Thank you," she said. She was blushing now and not able to look me in the face.

"How many times has Fred fucked you in that?" I asked.

"I said I didn't want to talk about Fred," she said.

"You know by now I get off on it," I said. "So how many times?"

Suzanne rolled her eyes. Then she said, "Three times. Valentine's day. His birthday. Our anniversary."

"Wow. All his special days," I teased with a mischievous grin. "That bustier must be really special to him. And now you're wearing it for me. Not being very nice to Freddy-boy."

"Clark god," Suzanne lamented. "Will you stop being such a dick and just fuck me? And will you stop calling him Freddy?"

I laughed.

Then I curled my finger at her. "Come closer Suzy," I said.

She walked to me until we almost touched. I curled my fingers in the top of her panties and pulled them down. I saw she had the beginnings of a thin landing strip, about an inch and a half long.

"Very sexy Suzy," I said as I rubbed her new landing strip with the flat of my thumb. Then I rubbed her clit. Suzanne moaned. Her pussy lips glistened with excitement. She was primed to be fucked.

"What will Freddy think?" I asked.

"I'll shave it off before he comes home," she said. Inwardly I grinned. She might do that, but not before Freddy-boy sees it.

God this was fun! I felt like an evil super-villain. Maybe I *was* Thanos.

"Come on," I said taking her hand. I led her downstairs to the basement.

"We're not going to your bedroom?" she asked, seeing the dusty, unfinished basement.

"You'll see," I said.

Earlier, I had put a mattress on the floor. "Lay there," I told her. "With your back propped up against the pillows."

Suzanne did as I told her, although she didn't understand what we were doing. "Give me your phone," I told her.

"Why?" she asked, looking warily at me.

"You'll find out in a second," I told her.

She hesitated, then reluctantly handed her phone to me.

"We're making a video for Freddy. That's why we're down here. He's been in my bedroom, he might recognize it," I told her. "You're going to look into the phone and tell Fred you miss him, you love him, and you're wearing the bustier that he loves, and you're sending him a special surprise. And then you're going to masturbate and make yourself cum."

"There's no way I'm making a sex tape you can post on the internet," Suzanne said indignantly.

"This is *your* phone Suzy. You're the only one who'll have the video," I told her. "And besides, don't you want Fred to jerk off to you instead of internet porn? I'm doing you a solid here."

"Fred doesn't look at internet porn."

"Yeah right," I said with a sarcastic laugh. I attached Suzanne's phone to a tripod so it was pointed towards her on the mattress.

"So why are you doing me a solid then?" she asked, eyeing me suspiciously.

"Because you're going to make this video for Freddy, and then I'm going to fuck your brains out in Freddy's favorite thing," I said with a laugh. "And I want to hear what you tell him about your new landing strip."

"Clark you are seriously evil," she said. I laughed again. She acted mad, but she didn't run away. Maybe she was turned on by this too. I figured sex with Fred was pretty vanilla. Boring. Maybe I *was* evil, but at least I wasn't boring.

I undid my pants and pulled out my cock.

"What are you doing?" Suzanne asked, looking at my man meat.

"I'm gonna stroke myself while you masturbate," I told her. "I wanna hear you tell Freddy you miss him and love him, when you know you're gonna cheat on his ass again as soon as the video is over."

"God Clark," Suzanne sighed, shaking her head. But her eyes were locked on my dick.

"You want this Suzy?" I asked her as I slowly stroked my shaft up and down.

Suzanne stared at my hard cock for a long moment more. Then she managed to tear her eyes away from my manhood. "Let's get this over with," she said scornfully.

I nodded and pressed the *record* button on her phone.

Suzanne looked directly at the phone and smiled. "Hey baby. It's me, your Suzy," she said. Her voice was suddenly very different. A moment ago, it was filled with anger and scorn. Now her voice was soft and loving. It was like she was a different person.

"I miss you so much Fred," she said. "And I love you so much. So I'm making this special video for you."

Suzanne ran her hands down her chest. "See? I'm wearing this thing you bought me for Valentine's Day. I know how much you love me in it. And I've done something really special for you."

Suzanne pulled her panties down her legs. Then she parted her thighs. Her new landing strip came into view.

"I know you like me completely bare, but I'm trying this out," she said. She ran the tip of her finger over the thin landing strip and said "Do you think it's sexy? If you don't, I'll shave it off. But I thought it would be fun to try it."

"I miss you so much babe," she cooed as she began to finger herself. "I miss your big cock so much. I can't wait until you're inside me again." As she said this, her eyes drifted to my cock as I stroked myself.

"I love how you make love to me," Suzanne said looking back into the phone. "I miss you so much babe."

Suzanne went on like this for about 5 minutes, fingering herself while saying loving things to her boyfriend. While most of the time she looked into her phone, more than a few times she sneaked peaks at me stroking my big cock.

Finally, she came. She said to me, "Okay, you can stop it." Her voice was back to how it was before the video. Harsh, terse, scornful.

I pressed the button on her phone to stop the recording.

Suzanne looked suspiciously around the room. She asked, "Do you have a camera somewhere? Recording this?"

"No," I said.

"You swear?"

"I swear," I told her. "I don't need to blackmail chicks since I've got this," I said, waving my big cock at her. She rolled her eyes at me.

Suzanne seemed to relax though. Then her eyes were back on my cock. I was still stroking myself.

"Is this how Fred beats off?" I asked. "With two hands?"

She looked at me but didn't say anything. I said, "I bet he only needs one hand to jerk his meat. Because his dick's small. And thin."

Suzanne's eyes were back on my cock. Still she didn't say anything.

"I bet he jerks off like this," I said. I moved one of my hands into the air. I formed a circle with my thumb and forefinger, and pumped up and down. "Is this how Freddy jerks off, Suzy? This is called circle jerking. You get it, right?"

Suzanne looked back at my face. I could tell from her eyes. She got it. And I was right. Freddy did circle jerk his little dick.

"You faked the orgasm," I said.

Still she didn't say anything.

"I bet you fake a lot of orgasms with Freddy," I said. "That's why you come back to me. Even though you hate my guts. I always make you cum on my cock."

I got on the mattress and kissed her. She didn't resist. She kissed me back. Her hands went to my cock, feeling and stroking my manhood. "You like my size, Suzy? You lied to Freddy when you said his cock is big. Maybe that's what you used to think. But now you know, right? After being with me. Now you know Freddy has a tiny pencil dick."

I got on top of Suzanne and pushed my cock into her. She groaned as I penetrated her.

I began to slowly fuck her. I pulled the top of the bustier down, freeing her big tits. I squeezed and caressed them as I moved in and out of her pussy.

"Do I fuck you better than Freddy?" I asked as I began fucking her harder.

She stared up at me. Her cheeks were flushed, and she was breathing hard. I could tell she was getting close to cumming.

"Tell me Suzy," I insisted as I fucked her hard. "Who fucks you better? Me or Fred?"

Finally, Suzanne relented and said, "You." The one word came out like a moan.

I leaned down and kissed her, pushing my tongue into her mouth. I ran my hands over the bustier. "From now on, whenever you wear this for Freddy, you're gonna be thinking of me," I hissed into her ear as I ran my hands up and down the sides of the bustier. "His little dick is gonna be inside you, but you're gonna be wishing it was my big cock instead."

A moment later, Suzanne cried out as she came. I was close behind, my orgasm fueled by all my nasty talk.

Just before exploding, I pulled out. I rapidly jerked myself to completion, shooting all of my jizz onto her Valentine's day bustier.

I took my mostly hard cock and used it like a paintbrush, spreading my cum all over the velvet of the red bustier. When I was done, I collapsed onto my back next to Suzanne, both of us panting hard.

After a few moments, Suzanne took off the bustier. She looked at it. When she saw it was wet from my sperm, she shook her head. She pulled off the stockings and began dressing.

"Stay," I said to her. "I've got pizza and beer."

She shook her head. "This is the last time Clark," she told me. She looked sad and regretful. "The things you say – the things you make me do – they're really mean. You're really mean, Clark."

A moment later, she was gone.

I went into the kitchen, still naked, my soft cock flapping around. I got a slice of pizza and opened a beer. I looked out the window as I ate, thinking about my new hobby.

What Suzanne said bothered me. But really, who was the bad guy here? She was the one cheating, not me. In fact, she was lucky it was me. I wasn't going to blab about fucking her. I wasn't trying to steal her away from Fred. And, I always got her off. She never had to fake an orgasm with me. She was lucky I was her fuck buddy and not some other dude who might truly be an asshole.

I was charged up about getting Suzanne to cheat on Fred again. And to wear the bustier, and grow a landing strip, and admit I was the better fuck. With each of those, she was betraying the man she loved. And it got me so fucking hot.

I was learning my kink wasn't just physical. Sticking my dick into another man's girl was just the start. I also loved the mind fuck.

Like, I wondered if I was messing with Suzanne's head about the size of Fred's dick. Would she view him the same way when he was home? Would she desire him the same way? Would she enjoy sex with him as much?

Or had I turned her into a size queen? Did she now think of Fred's penis as a boy's little dick?

These thoughts got me hot, and my cock began stiffening even as I grabbed another beer and slice of pepperoni pizza. I thought about rubbing one out, but then decided to save it.

I didn't know what would happen when I saw Molly next, but I wanted my libido and my balls to be fully charged up, just in case.

<hr>

In the future, looking back, I realized I should have paid more attention to what Suzanne said. At the time, I was thinking only with my dick, and my ego. I was all about getting into the pants of girls who belonged to other men.

But actions have consequences. Often bad consequences. Especially with the shit I was doing. The problem was, I only figured that out later.

CHAPTER 7

"You're a real psycho," Molly angrily said as soon as she opened the door. "What would have happened if Johnny found what you left? Did you think about that?"

In fact, I hadn't thought about that. I mean, what dude goes through his wife's lingerie drawer? I figured honestly was the best way out of this mess. "No, I didn't think about that," I said looking regretful. "I'm sorry."

Molly eyed me. Maybe me caving immediately calmed her anger, at least a little. She said, "Well, I'm keeping the forty dollars this week. It's going to cost at least that much to get everything dry cleaned."

"It costs forty bucks to clean panties?" I asked, shocked.

Molly rolled her eyes. "My wedding dress, dumb shit," she said irritably. "I can't stand knowing you touched it. And I have to buy a new frame for my wedding picture. You ruined it."

"So just go," Molly said, dismissively waving her hand towards the lawn behind me. "Go cut the grass, you pervert."

As I cut the grass, I was upbeat. Molly didn't slap my face. She didn't tell me to go fuck myself. She didn't fire me. All she did was tell me to cut the grass, which I was gonna do anyway.

When I was done and returned to the kitchen with the 2 batteries, Molly was there. "Go ahead and put them in," she said. "I can never figure out how to slide them in."

I put the batteries into their chargers. When I turned around, Molly was still there, looking at me.

"Here," she said, throwing the Titan 3XL condom at me. "If you ever do something like that again, I'll tell your parents."

"You know why it's XL?" I said.

"What?" Molly asked, not understanding.

"It's not the length," I said. "You don't need the condom to go all the way down your shaft. It's the thickness. That's why I need 3XL. Anything smaller and it'll rip when I try to roll it down my cock."

"TMI," Molly said with a laugh. It was a nervous laugh, and her cheeks were flushed.

"Don't you want to know why I did what I did?" I asked.

"No, I don't want to know," Molly said with the nervous laugh again.

"I saw your wedding picture. And then I found your wedding dress. And then I couldn't help myself," I told her.

Molly was looking at me. She asked "Why couldn't you help yourself?"

Molly was fishing for compliments, and that's when I realized what was going on. Despite her obvious beauty, her husband was taking her for granted. And in our small, conservative beach town, she didn't get much male attention. Given how hot she was, if she lived in New York City or some other big city, guys would be hitting on her all the time. But not here in our sleepy beach town. Here, you don't hit on a girl if her husband is your friend. Unless you're a freako like me.

I moved closer and ran my fingertips down her cheek. "You were a gorgeous bride," I said. "You're still gorgeous. Even more beautiful now."

Molly grabbed my hand. "It'll ruin my life if my husband ever finds out," she said.

"He'll never find out," I said. Then I pulled her into my arms and kissed her.

⸺⊛⸺

Sex with Molly was exquisite for lot of reasons.

First, I was pretty sure she was the prettiest girl I'd ever been with. Looking down into her gorgeous face as I fucked her was out of this world. Looking at her face when she came was practically a life changing experience.

Second, her body was so tight, even after having 2 kids. Whatever they did in those Pilates classes, it sure was working. Also, her little A cup tits were amazing. Some dudes like big breasts (like Suzanne's), but I'll take perky tiny tits anytime.

Third, her legs and ass were fantastic. They should hire her for Vanna's gig once she retires.

And finally – most of all – fucking a wife was a lot hotter than fucking a girlfriend. Looking at Molly's engagement and wedding rings as she came on my cock was so fucking hot!

As I suspected, Molly told me her husband wasn't paying attention to her like he used to. What an idiot! She felt neglected and lonely, and that's what led her into my arms (and why she opened her legs for me).

It didn't hurt that she got off on my young, beach body. And my big cock. I didn't push it the way I had with Suzanne, but I could tell I fucked her better than her husband Johnny. Often after she came, she looked at me in awe and amazement, like she was saying "what did you just do to me?"

So my first affair with a married woman began. We fucked every Wednesday, except on those rare occasions when her kids didn't have their regular playdate.

Our affair was limited to those Wednesday hookups, until her country club hired my restaurant to cater its mid-summer party.

The week before during our Wednesday hookup, I gave her a present. Molly's jaw dropped. Inside were *Jimmy Choo* high heels.

"Clark I can't accept this," she said. "It must have cost so much money."

In fact, they *had* cost a ton of money. Almost a full week of tips. But I figured, if I bought her expensive ones, she would wear them.

"Your legs are so fantastic, they deserve expensive high heels," I said with a grin.

Molly blushed. She loved getting compliments. Her husband was an idiot for focusing so much on his career instead of his wife.

"I'm not sure I can walk in these," she said with a laugh. The shiny black Jimmy Choos had 4 ½ inch stiletto heels. I knew she normally wore 2 inch princess heels. And these shoes had a name – who would have known shoes had names? They were called *Romy 100*.

"It'll get me hot seeing you wearing these shoes," I told her.

She looked warily at me. "Clark, nothing can happen at the party," she warned me. "I'll be with Johnny. And I'll know everyone there. You'll probably know them too."

"I won't try anything," I said. I wasn't being honest. But I wasn't going to force her to do anything.

I actually liked Molly. Even though she was 35 years old, she was still naïve. She didn't realize how pretty and sexy she was. She'd had sex with a few men – she told me less than five – and none since she began dating Johnny in high school (except for me).

So for the most part, her sexual life was limited to her husband Johnny. And while he might be a smart lawyer, in bed he was plain brown vanilla. Sexually, I took her places she didn't know existed.

You might wonder why Molly fell into my arms. Why, after being faithful to Johnny their entire marriage, she was now having an affair. Why she was cheating on her husband.

Well, like I said, Johnny wasn't giving her attention like he had when they were younger, before the kids, and before he got obsessed with making partner at his law firm.

Also, Molly told me when she turned 35, it freaked her out. She was now middle age and she had never done anything exciting in her life.

Molly had always been a good girl. So, when I ran into her that time in the parking lot of the restaurant, she had been primed to do something naughty. She didn't realize it at the time. She just needed a push. And I pushed her.

The fact she was having an affair with me – a boy almost half her age – was scandalous to her. And that's exactly what she wanted – she wanted to break out of the mold of being a good girl, and be naughty and exciting for once in her life.

"Can you do something for me though?" I asked. I was always nice and deferential to Molly. I sensed that's what she wanted. She was 35 and I was 18. She was the adult and I was the boy. That fed into her desire to be bad. To her, there was nothing more wicked than to have an affair with a teenage boy, so that's how I acted.

"Can you wear stockings at the party? I'll be hard all night seeing you in stockings and these high heels."

"Well, it'll be hot wearing hose in the summer," Molly said with a grin. "But why not? The club is air conditioned."

I smiled at her thankfully. Then I gently said, "I was also wondering ... the night before the party is Johnny's birthday. Right? His birthday is your door code. 0807. Right?"

"Right ...," Molly said, the one word coming out like a question

"Wanna have some fun?" I said with a mischievous grin. "Don't have sex with him that night."

"But ... we always have sex on his birthday," Molly said looking uncertain.

"It'll get me hot knowing he's got blue balls at the club party," I said with a boyish grin. "And anyway, you can make it up to him after the party. He'll probably be super horny seeing you running around all night in the stockings and heels."

"Well ... I guess I can do that," Molly said, still looking uncertain.

I felt triumphant inside! Once again I felt like an evil super-villain!

But I played it cool. I never went alpha asshole on Molly, the way I acted with Suzanne. That would burst the bubble of me being a lovestruck teenaged boy.

Instead, I said admiringly, "I can't wait to see you in a dress and those heels. And stockings. You're gonna look so beautiful."

Molly smiled shyly and adorably brushed a lock of blond hair behind her ear. Like I said, she loved compliments.

"You're so hot Molly," I said as I kissed her neck and got on top of her.

"Already?" Molly said with an amazed laugh. We'd fucked just before I gave her the Jimmy Choos, and I was hard again.

"You're so hot Molly," I said again, kissing her neck below her ear the way I knew she loved it. I was laying it on thick to feed into her insecurities. "I can never get enough of your sexy body."

"Oh god," she moaned as I nuzzled her neck.

"Besides it gets me hot I'm with a MILF," I said.

Molly laughed, but it came out like a moan.

I pushed my cock into her. She grunted as my big cock stretched her.

"You like how I feel Molly?" I asked as I pushed more of myself into her.

"Yeah, yeah ...," she moaned as she clenched her eyes shut. She always did that when I first entered her.

"You're so tight Molly," I said as I kissed her. I was fully inside her now, and I began moving in and out. "Johnny hasn't stretched you out."

"I always thought he was big," Molly said, breathing hard. "Until I met you."

I got so charged up when she said things like that! My cock jerked inside her.

Molly felt it and smiled. She said, "You like hearing you're bigger than my husband."

"Yeah, I do," I admitted. I kissed her again, and she kissed me back. We continued kissing and touching each other until we both came.

<hr>

Molly looked incredible in the high heels and stockings. She even wore an above-the-knee dress, which for her was pretty racy. I wondered if she had bought it special for his party.

At a buffet party like this, I had a few jobs. Bartender. Walking around serving hors d'oeuvres and glasses of champagne. Re-filling buffet trays.

It was when I was bartending that she approached me. We were alone for a moment so I took my time making her dirty martini. "You look fucking amazing in that dress," I whispered to her.

She tried to hide a smile in case anyone was watching, but I could tell she was flattered. "Thanks," she whispered back.

"How did last night go?" I whispered.

"Johnny wasn't happy," she said in a low voice. But she had a hint of a smile on her very pretty face. "I told him I had a headache."

"Maybe if he bought you stiletto heels sometimes, he'd get lucky more often," I whispered. This time she couldn't help a stifled laugh.

"When was the last time you came?" I asked. "And I mean, not from your own hand."

"Oh my god. I can't believe the conversations I have with you," she said, a grin in her voice if not on her face.

"When?" I pressed.

"Last week with you," she whispered.

"So Johnny doesn't do you as good as me?" I asked with a grin.

"You'd love it if I said he doesn't, right?" Molly said. Now she was openly grinning back at me.

"Yes," I admitted. She laughed.

She took the dirty martini and turned to go. I asked, "Did you buy that dress for me?"

Over her shoulder, she gave me a smile but didn't say anything.

As the evening progressed, I made a couple of drinks for Johnny. Without him knowing, I made them extra strong. He clearly wasn't a drinker as I could tell he was tipsy.

The band began playing dancing songs and the lights dimmed. People crowded onto the dance floor. I saw Johnny laughing and talking with some buddies.

I approached Molly and whispered "You know where the manager's office is? Meet me there."

"Are you crazy?" Molly whispered back, nervously searching the crowd for her husband.

"Everybody's half looped. Johnny's drunk. No one will notice you're gone."

"Clark, no way," Molly said with that nervous look on her pretty face.

"Do you want to wait until Wednesday to get fucked good?" I asked her. "Come on. I only need 5 minutes and you'll be cumming hard on my cock."

A few minutes later we were in the manager's office. It was down the hall from the ballroom so I knew we had privacy.

"God I want you," I said as I took Molly into my arms and kissed her. I knew we didn't have time for foreplay.

I turned her around so her front was against the manager's desk. I bent her over and, at the same time, pulled up the skirt of her dress.

I took a moment to look at her. Fuck her long legs looked so good in those thigh high stockings! And her tight ass was amazing in her thong panties!

I didn't even bother to take off her panties. I just pulled them aside and then pushed my hard cock into her.

I immediately started fucking her hard. I moved one of my hands to her front and squeezed and fondled her little tits over her dress and bra. With my other hand, I rubbed her clit while I fucked her from behind. We only had a few minutes so I was using all my tricks to make her cum fast.

And Molly did cum fast. After another couple minutes of getting fucked hard and having her clit fingered, she exploded on my cock. She bit into her arm to stifle her moans.

Now that I had gotten her off, I let myself go. I'd gotten Molly to cheat on her husband again, this time at a party with all her friends and her husband just footsteps away. It was fucking hot! There was no way I could hold off blowing my load!

I tightly grabbed Molly's hips so I could get as deep as possible. I thrusted hard into her pussy, once, twice, three times, each time ejaculating my sperm into her womb.

When we were done, we were both grinning, like little kids who had done something naughty. And we had been naughty. I'd just fucked a married girl with her husband not 50 feet away from us. And once again, I proved to Molly I fucked her better than Johnny. He might be twice as old as me, but when it came to sex, I was the man, and he was the boy.

Molly hurriedly pushed her dress down, then fixed her hair and makeup. "How do I look?" she asked.

"You look very fuckable," I told her with a grin. She grinned back at me.

"Do you think Johnny is gonna want to fuck you tonight?" I asked.

"Don't ask me to deny him again Clark," Molly said. "He's my husband."

"I'm not gonna ask that," I said. "But he's drunk."

"So?"

"So make him eat you out first, before he fucks you," I said. I was wearing a mischievous smile.

It took Molly a moment to get it. Because she was a good girl, and the idea had never occurred to her.

But when she finally got it, her lips parted in surprise. I was asking her to get Johnny to eat out the creampie I'd just deposited in her.

"God Clark that's really bad," she said with a hint of a smile. She turned to go but I grabbed her hand.

"You'll be alone Wednesday, right? Because a quickie isn't enough. I want more time with you."

"Clark ...," Molly said, shyly brushing a lock of blonde hair behind her ear. I loved when she did that. It was so cute and adorable.

"I'll make sure the kids have their playdate," she promised.

As she turned to go again, I said "Hey Molly?"

"Yeah?"

"When I get there Wednesday, wear those high heels," I said. "And nothing else."

"Oh my god Clark," she said with a laugh. With a delighted twinkle in her pretty blue eyes, she turned and went back to her husband in the ballroom.

———◉———

CONTINUED IN
GIRLS WHO BELONG TO OTHER MEN
BOOK 2

———◉———

Available at Amazon Kindle and Smashwords.

Don't miss out!

Visit the website below and you can sign up to receive emails whenever Pete Andrews publishes a new book. There's no charge and no obligation.

https://books2read.com/r/B-A-KWSAB-GSUOC

BOOKS 2 READ

Connecting independent readers to independent writers.